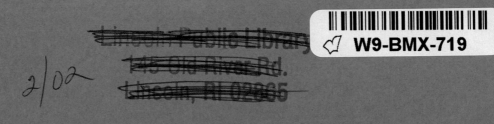
W9-BMX-719

The Pie Is Cherry

Michael Rex

Henry Holt and Company • New York

To Karen S.,
who likes chocolate, too.

Henry Holt and Company, LLC, *Publishers since 1866*
115 West 18th Street, New York, New York 10011

Henry Holt is a registered trademark
of Henry Holt and Company, LLC

Copyright © 2001 by Michael Rex
All rights reserved.
Published in Canada by Fitzhenry & Whiteside Ltd.,
195 Allstate Parkway, Markham, Ontario L3R 4T8.

Library of Congress Cataloging-in-Publication Data
Rex, Michael.
The pie is cherry / Michael Rex.
Summary: Text and pictures describe things in a kitchen from utensils to food.
[1. Kitchens—Fiction. 2. Vocabulary.] I. Title.
PZ7.R32875 Pi 2001   [E]—dc21   00-57506

ISBN 0-8050-6717-5
First Edition—2001
Printed in the United States of America on acid-free paper. ∞
1 3 5 7 9 10 8 6 4 2

The artist created the illustrations for this book in pencil;
color was added using Adobe® Graphic Software.

The napkins are paper.
The straw is bendy.
The ice is frozen.
The soda is bubbly.
The sandwich is cut.

The popcorn
is popping!

The bags are plastic.

The milk is spilled.

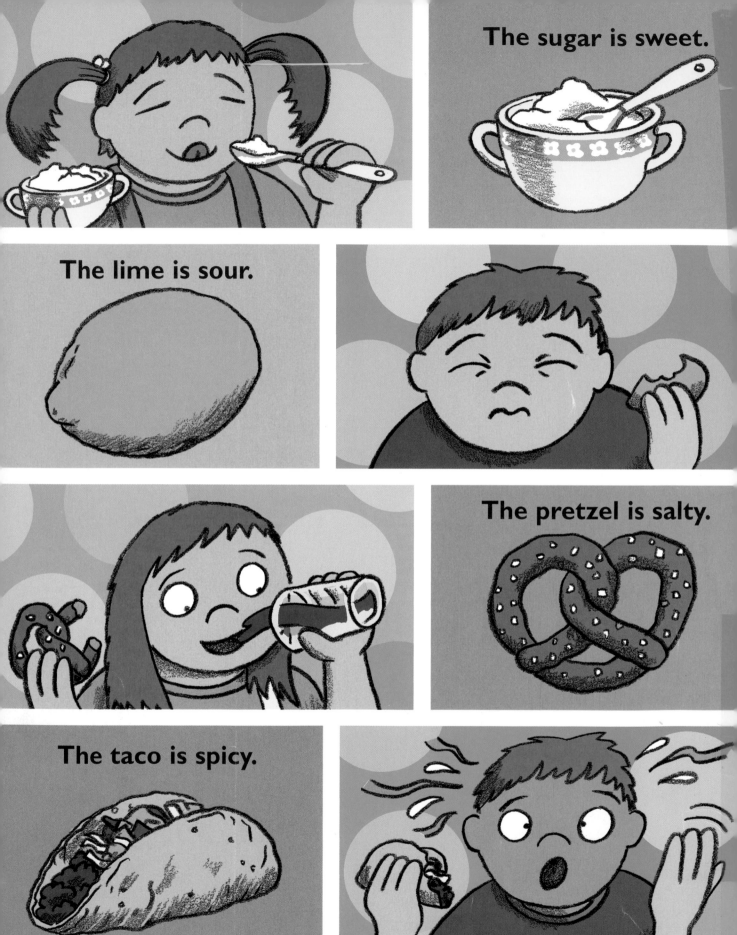

The sugar is sweet.

The lime is sour.

The pretzel is salty.

The taco is spicy.

The box is square.

The pizza is round.

The slice is triangular.

The tray is rectangular.

The cookies are oatmeal.

The watermelon is big.

The raisin is small.

The tomato is ripe.

The pots are banged.
The pans are clanged.

COOK BOOK

The stove is hot.

The chicken is baked.
The beef is broiled.

The recipe is followed.
The mitt is worn.
The batter is mixed.
The ham is glazed.
The corn is shucked.
The pasta is boiled.

The table is set.   **The soup is steamy.**

The steak is juicy.

The potatoes are mashed.

The spaghetti is squiggly.

The bread is warm.

The turkey is stuffed.

The cake
is chocolate.

The pudding is butterscotch.

The milkshake is vanilla.

The ice cream is strawberry.

The cream is whipped.

The pie is cherry,

and it sure is yummy!